Praise for

# Akimbo

A Book Sense Children's Pick

"Akimbo is a very brave little boy who keeps his wits about him even when he's being stalked by a rhino."
—*The New York Times Book Review*

"Satisfying page-turners that celebrate kids' curiosity, love of adventure, and capacity to care for the world they inhabit." —*Parenting* magazine

"The tale's brevity, Smith's concise writing and Pham's evocative full-page half-tone illustrations make this an attractive choice for reluctant readers."
—*Publishers Weekly*

"Akimbo emerges as a brave, caring protagonist who faces dilemmas and danger in the service of the animals and people he loves." —*Booklist*

"The African setting, dramatic full-page pencil illustrations, and the animal facts woven into the stories are sure to capture young readers." —*SLJ*

"[These] gently told yet exciting stories reveal another side of McCall Smith's love for Africa, championing the importance of wild animals amid threats to their survival." —*Chicago Sun-Times*

"Smith captures the essence of his beloved Africa in the same manner as that which has made his adult 'No. 1 Ladies' Detective Agency' series so popular."
—*Monterey County Herald*

ALEXANDER McCALL SMITH

# AKIMBO and the ELEPHANTS

ILLUSTRATED BY LeUyen Pham

BLOOMSBURY
CHILDREN'S
BOOKS

*This book is for*
*Alan and Barbara Hannah,*
*and for Jeremy and Kathryn*

Text copyright © 1990 by Alexander McCall Smith
Illustrations copyright © 2005 by LeUyen Pham
Originally published in 1990 in the U.K. by Mammoth,
an imprint of Mandarin Paperbacks
Mandarin is an imprint of the Octopus Publishing Group
Published in 2005 in the U.S. by Bloomsbury U.S.A. Children's Books
Paperback edition published in 2007

Published by Bloomsbury U.S.A. Children's Books
175 Fifth Avenue, New York, NY 10010
Distributed to the trade by Holtzbrinck Publishers

The Library of Congress has cataloged the hardcover edition as follows:
McCall Smith, Alexander.
Akimbo and the elephants / by Alexander McCall Smith ;
illustrated by LeUyen Pham. —1st U.S. ed.
p. cm.
Summary: On the African game preserve where his father works, Akimbo
devises a dangerous plan to capture a ring of elephant poachers.
ISBN-13: 978-1-58234-686-1 • ISBN-10: 1-58234-686-0 (hardcover)
[1. Elephants—Fiction. 2. Poaching—Fiction. 3. Game reserves—Fiction.
4. Africa—Fiction.] I. Pham, LeUyen, ill. II. Title.
PZ7.M47833755Akm 2005 [Fic]—dc22 2005043620

ISBN-13: 978-1-59990-031-5 • ISBN-10: 1-59990-031-9 (paperback)

Typeset by Hewer Text UK Ltd, Edinburgh
Printed in the U.S.A. by Worzalla
1 3 5 7 9 10 8 6 4 2

All papers used by Bloomsbury U.S.A. are natural, recyclable products made
from wood grown in well-managed forests. The manufacturing processes
conform to the environmental regulations of the country of origin.

# CONTENTS

# Akimbo's Wish

Imagine living in the heart of Africa. Imagine living in a place where the sun rises each morning over blue mountains and great plains with grass that grows taller than a man. Imagine living in a place where there are still elephants.

Akimbo lived in such a place, on the edge of a large game reserve in Africa. This was a place where wild animals could live in safety. On its plains there were great herds of antelope and zebra. In the forests and in the rocky hills there were leopards and baboons. And, of course, there were the great elephants, who roamed slowly across the grasslands and among the trees.

1

Akimbo's father worked here. Sometimes he drove trucks; sometimes he manned the radio or helped to repair the trucks. There was always something to do.

If Akimbo was lucky, his father would occasionally take him with him to work. Akimbo loved to go with the men when they went off deep into the reserve. They might have to mend a game fence or rescue a broken-down truck, or it might just be a routine patrol through the forest to check up on the animals.

Sometimes on these trips, they would see something exciting.

"Look over there," his father would say. "Don't make a noise. Just look over there."

And Akimbo would follow his father's gaze and see some wild creature eating, or resting, or crouching in wait for its prey.

One day, when they were walking through the forest together, Akimbo's father suddenly seized his arm and whispered to him to be still.

"What is it?" Akimbo made his voice as soft as he could manage.

"Walk backward. Very slowly. Go back the way we came."

It was only as he began to inch back that Akimbo realized what had happened. There in a clearing not far away were two leopards. One of them, sensing that something was happening, had risen to its feet and was sniffing at the air. The other was still sleeping.

Luckily, the wind was blowing in the wrong direction, or the leopard would have smelled their presence. If that had happened, then they would have been in even greater danger.

"That was close," his father said, once they had gotten away. "I don't like to think what would have happened if I hadn't noticed them in time."

It was not leopards, or even lions, that Akimbo liked to watch. He loved the elephants best of all. You had to keep clear of them, too, but they seemed more gentle than many of the other creatures. Akimbo loved their vast, lumbering shapes. He loved the way they moved their trunks slowly, this way and that,

as they plodded across the plains between the stretches of forest. And he loved the sound of an elephant trumpeting—a short, surprised, rather funny sound.

There used to be many elephants in Africa, but over the years they had been mercilessly hunted. Now there were fewer and fewer.

Akimbo could not understand why anybody should want to hunt an elephant and asked his father why.

"It's for their tusks. They're made of ivory, and ivory is very valuable. It's used for ornaments and jewelry. Some rich people collect it and like to show off elephant tusks carved into fancy shapes."

"But it's so cruel," said Akimbo. "I'm glad it doesn't happen anymore."

Akimbo's father was silent for a moment.

"I'm afraid it does still happen. There are still people who hunt elephants—even here in the reserve."

"Can't you stop them?" he asked.

Akimbo's father shook his head. "It's very difficult. The reserve stretches for almost a hundred miles. We can't keep an eye on all of it all the time."

Akimbo was silent. The thought of the elephants being hunted for their tusks made him seethe with anger. He wondered whether there would come a day when all the elephants in Africa were destroyed. Then all that we would have to remember them by would be photographs and, of course, the ivory from their tusks. The reserves would be empty then, and the sight of the elephants crossing the plains would be nothing but a memory.

"I don't want that to happen," Akimbo said to himself. "I want the elephants to stay."

# FATHER ELEPHANT

A few weeks later, Akimbo was to be reminded of what his father had said about the poachers.

"We have to go out to check up on a water hole," his father said. "Do you want to come with us?"

"Yes," said Akimbo eagerly.

"It'll be a rough ride," his father warned him. "There isn't even a road for much of the way."

"I don't mind. I know how to hang on."

Akimbo's father was right. It was not an easy journey, and it was very hot as well. At noon the sun burned down unmercifully, and it was unbearably hot in the truck cabin.

Akimbo wiped the sweat off his face and drank great gulps of water from the water bottles, but he did not complain once.

They had to travel slowly, as there were rocks and potholes which could easily damage the truck if they came upon them too quickly. Every now and then, a concealed rock would scrape against the bottom of the truck with a painful, jarring sound, and everybody inside would wince. But no damage was done, and they continued their journey.

During the hot hours of midday, few animals will venture out of the shade of the trees and the undergrowth. But Akimbo saw a small herd of zebra cantering off to safety, throwing up a cloud of dust behind them.

Then, quite suddenly, one of the men in the back of the truck hit his fist on the top of the roof and pointed off to the left. Akimbo's father brought the vehicle to a halt.

"What is it?" he called out.

The man leaned over into the cabin.

"Vultures. Flocks of them."

The eyes of all the others followed the

man's gaze. Akimbo saw nothing at first, but when he craned his neck he saw the birds circling in the hot, still air. Even from this distance, he could tell that there were lots of them, and so he knew that something big was attracting their attention.

Akimbo's father turned to one of the other men.

"Do you think the lions finished a meal?"

The other man looked thoughtful. "Maybe. But there are rather a lot of vultures for that. Don't you think we should go and take a look?"

Akimbo's father agreed. Then, swinging the truck off to the left, he steered in the direction of the circling birds. After a bumpy ride of fifteen minutes they were there, and they saw the sad sight that they had all secretly been dreading.

The elephant lay on its side, where it had fallen. As the truck approached, four or five vultures flapped up into the air, angry at the disturbance of their feeding. Akimbo's father looked furious as he drew the truck to a halt.

Without speaking, he opened his door and strode off to stand beside the fallen elephant.

Akimbo stayed where he was. He could not bear to look at the great creature. He knew that the elephant had been destroyed so that its tusks could be stolen.

Akimbo looked away. There was a group of trees nearby, and as Akimbo looked toward it he noticed movement. Then, a little way away, the vegetation moved.

Akimbo strained his eyes to try to see more. He was sure an animal was there, but it was difficult to see through the thick covering of leaves and branches. He hoped it was not a buffalo, which could be dangerous.

There was another movement, and this time Akimbo was looking in the right place. Quickly opening the door of the truck cabin, Akimbo leapt out and ran to where his father and the other men were standing.

"Look!" he cried out. "Look over there!"

The men spun around. As they did so, the baby elephant broke cover. It took a few steps and then stopped, as if uncertain what to do. It raised its trunk and sniffed at the air. Then it dropped its trunk and stood quite still. Akimbo noticed that it had a torn right ear.

"It's her calf," said his father. "It's very young."

They stared at the calf for a few moments. The tiny elephant was obviously confused. It saw its mother lying motionless on the ground, and it wanted to join her. At the same time, its instinct told it to keep away from the intruding men.

"Can we look after it?" Akimbo asked.

Akimbo's father shook his head. "No. The herd will pick it up. If we leave it here, another cow elephant will come for it."

"But it's so small. Can't we take it back to the compound and look after it?"

"It will be all right," said Akimbo's father. "It's best not to interfere."

They began to walk back to the truck. At a distance, the little elephant watched them go, withdrawing slightly as they moved. When the engine started, Akimbo saw it run back to the shelter of the trees.

"Good-bye," Akimbo muttered under his breath. "Good luck."

The truck turned away. Akimbo took one last glance back and saw that the vultures, which had been circling high in the sky, had now dropped lower.

# STOLEN IVORY

Over the next few days, Akimbo found himself thinking more and more about the baby elephant. He wondered whether it had been picked up by another member of the herd, or whether it had been left to die. Had the poachers destroyed two elephants in their cruel and greedy hunt for ivory?

He knew that his father and the other game rangers were doing their best to stop the hunters, but they seemed unable to deal with them.

"If I were in charge," he said to himself, "I'd catch them and teach them a lesson. If nobody else will, then I'm going to stop them."

He thought about this. There was no reason why the poachers should get away with it. Perhaps there was something he could do, after all.

"Where do the poachers come from?" he asked his father one evening.

His father shrugged his shoulders. "From all over the place. But we know that there's one gang in the village nearby. We can't prove it, but we think they're doing it."

"What do they do with the tusks?" Akimbo asked.

His father sighed. "They hide them. Traders come up from the towns and buy them from them. Then they smuggle the tusks back to town and that's where they're carved. They make them into necklaces and ornaments."

"But don't you ever catch any of them?"

"Sometimes. Then we hand them over to the police. But the poachers are cunning, and clever as well."

Akimbo turned away. "I'm clever too," he muttered under his breath. "And I'm sure I can be as cunning as they are."

"What was that?" his father asked.

"Nothing," Akimbo replied. But he had declared war on the poachers the moment he saw that baby elephant waiting in vain for its mother to get up.

Akimbo knew that it would be impossible for him to do anything about the poachers in the reserve itself. The poaching gangs traveled by night and were armed. Then they struck as quickly and quietly as possible before fading away into the bush again. Every so often, the rangers picked up their tracks and pursued them, but usually they were too late.

He thought of different plans, but none of them seemed likely to work. If there was no point in waiting for the poachers, why not go to the village and find them? That was the way to get the proof he needed to stop them.

At the edge of the rangers' camp was a storeroom. Akimbo had been inside only once or twice, as it was always kept locked, and his father rarely went there. In it were the things the rangers confiscated from poachers when they managed to find them.

It was a grim collection. There were cruel barbed-wire traps, designed to tighten like a noose around an animal's leg when it stepped into the concealed circle of wire. There were rifles, spears, and ammunition belts. But what was saddest of all were the parts of animals which had been caught by the poachers. As well as horns and skins, there were the most sought-after trophies of all, the tusks of elephants.

Many of these things were kept to show to visitors, so that they could see what the poachers did. Some were also kept in the hope they would be needed as evidence once the poachers were caught. But that seemed to happen so rarely that the tusks and the traps just gathered more and more dust.

That night, when the rest of the camp was asleep, Akimbo slipped out of his room and made his way across the compound toward the storeroom. In the moonlight he could make out the shape of the storeroom against

the night sky. He paused in the shadows for a few moments to check that nobody was near-by, and then he darted along the path to stand in front of the storeroom door.

His father's bunch of keys was heavy in his pocket. He had slipped it out of the pocket of his father's working tunic while his parents were busy in the kitchen. He had felt bad about that, but he told himself that he was not stealing anything for himself.

Now he tried each key in the storeroom lock. It was a slow business. In spite of the moonlight, there was still not enough light to see clearly, and it was difficult to keep the keys he had already used from being jumbled up with those he had yet to try. At one point he dropped the whole bunch, and it made a loud, jangly noise, but nobody woke up.

At last the lock moved, and with a final twist the bolt slid home. Akimbo pushed open the door and wrinkled his nose as he smelled the familiar, rotten odor of the un-cured skins. But it was not skins he had come for. There, in a corner, was a small elephant tusk, which had been roughly sawn in two.

Akimbo picked this up, checked that it was not too heavy to carry, and took it out of the storeroom. He took off its label. Then, locking the door again, he crept away, just like a poacher making off with his load of stolen ivory.

# THE ENEMY

"I'd like to go to the village," Akimbo told his parents the following morning.

Akimbo's father seemed surprised.

"Why? There's nothing for you to do there."

'There's Mato. I haven't seen him for a long time. I'd like to see him. Last time I was there, his aunt said that I could stay with them for a few days."

His father shrugged his shoulders, looking at Akimbo's mother.

"If you want to go, I suppose you can," she said. "You'll have to walk there, though. It'll take three hours—maybe more. And don't be any trouble for Mato's aunt."

Again Akimbo felt bad. He did not like to lie to his parents, but if he told them of his plan, he was sure that they would prevent him from trying it out. And if that happened, then nobody would ever stop the poachers, and the hunting of the elephants would go on and on.

As his mother had warned him, the walk was not easy. And, carrying a chunk of ivory in a sack over his shoulder, Akimbo found it even more difficult than he had imagined. Every few minutes he had to stop and rest, sliding the sack off his shoulder and waiting for his tired arm muscles to recover. Then he would heave the sack up again and continue his walk, keeping away from the main path to avoid meeting anybody.

At last the village was in sight. Akimbo did not go straight in, but looked around in the bush for a hiding place. Eventually he found an old termite hole. He stuffed the sack in it and placed a few dead branches over the top. It was the perfect place.

Once in the village, he went straight to Mato's house. Mato lived with his aunt.

She was a nurse and ran the small clinic at the edge of the village. Mato was surprised to see Akimbo, but pleased, and took him in for a cup of water in the kitchen.

"I need your help," said Akimbo to his friend. "I want to find somebody who will buy some ivory from me."

Mato's eyes opened wide with surprise.

"But where did you get it?" he stuttered. "Did you steal it?"

Akimbo shook his head. Then, swearing his friend to secrecy, he told him his plan. Mato thought for awhile and then he gave him his opinion.

"It won't work," he said flatly. "You'll just get into trouble. That's all that will happen."

Akimbo shook his head. "I'm ready to take that risk."

So Mato, rather reluctantly, told Akimbo about a man in the village whom everyone thought was dishonest.

"If I had stolen something that I wanted to sell," he said, "I'd go to him. He's called Matimba, and I can show you where he lives.

But I'm not going into his house. You'll have to go in on your own."

Matimba was not there the first time that Akimbo went to the house. When he returned an hour later, though, he was told to wait at the back door. After ten minutes or so, the door opened and a stout man with a beard looked out.

"Yes?" he said, his voice curt and suspicious.

"I would like to speak to you," Akimbo said politely.

"Then speak," snapped Matimba.

Akimbo looked over his shoulder.

"I have something to sell. I thought you might like it."

Matimba laughed. "*You* sell something to *me*?"

Akimbo ignored the laughter. "Yes. Here it is."

When he saw the ivory tusk sticking out of the top of Akimbo's sack, Matimba stopped laughing. "Come inside. And bring that with you."

Inside the house, Akimbo was told to sit on a chair while Matimba examined the tusk. He looked at it under the light, sniffed it, and rubbed at it with his forefinger. Then he laid it down on a table and stared at Akimbo.

"Where did you get this?" he asked.

"I found it," said Akimbo. "I found a whole lot of tusks. And some rhino horns."

At the mention of rhino horns, Matimba narrowed his eyes. These horns were much in demand among smugglers, and they could fetch very high prices on the coast. If this boy has really got some, Matimba thought, I could get them off him for next to nothing.

"Where did you find them?"

"In a hiding place near a river. I think they must have been hidden there by a poacher who got caught and couldn't come back for them."

Matimba nodded. This sort of thing did happen, and now this innocent boy had stumbled across a fortune. He looked at the tusk again. He would give him some money on the spot and promise him more if he took him to the rest.

"You did well to come to me. I can buy these things from you."

Akimbo drew in his breath. Now was the time for him to make his demand. "You can have them. I don't want money for them."

Matimba was astonished. He looked again at the boy and wondered whether there was something wrong with him.

"All I want is to become an elephant hunter. If you let me go off with some poachers—to learn how they do it—I'll show you where I have hidden the tusks and horns."

Matimba was silent. He stared at Akimbo for some time, wondering whether to trust him. Then his greed got the better of his caution. He granted Akimbo's wish. After all, boys thought poaching was exciting. Well, let him learn.

"You may go with my men," he said.

Akimbo felt a great surge of excitement. Matimba had said "my men." He had found the head of a gang of poachers. His plan had worked—so far. The next stage was the really dangerous part.

# THE HUNT

**M**atimba told Akimbo to come back the following night. He was to bring nothing with him and expect to be away for two or three days. The men would bring the food.

"I hope that you're strong enough," he said dubiously. "And I hope your parents won't come looking for you."

Akimbo reassured him, but Matimba was no longer paying attention. He had picked up the tusk again and was polishing its surface with a cloth. Akimbo threw a last glance at it before he left the room. He hoped that the loss of the tusk would not be noticed too soon. He would have to own up to taking it, but he wanted to only when his plan had been carried out. If it failed, then he did not look forward to confessing that he had given the tusk to the head of a poaching gang.

Mato was still worried. As they lay side by side on their sleeping mats, Mato told Akimbo, "You're crazy. Go straight home and tell your father what you've done."

Akimbo told him about how they had found the baby elephant, waiting for its mother.

"We can't let all the elephants of Africa be destroyed. I must do something for them."

Mato was silent at the end of Akimbo's story. "All right. I suppose I should say good luck."

"Thank you," said Akimbo. Then, feeling tired after the day's long walk, he drifted off to sleep, not hearing the sound of the village dogs barking or the whine of the crickets outside. Mato stayed awake a little longer worrying about his friend, but at last he, too, fell asleep.

The next day dragged past with a painful slowness. At last, as the sun began to sink below the hills, Akimbo knew that it was time for him to go to Matimba's house. He was the only person there to begin with, but a little while later several men arrived. They looked suspiciously at Akimbo, and spoke in lowered voices to Matimba. After that, they appeared to accept Akimbo's presence.

There were five men in the group. The leader was a short man who walked with a limp. He gave orders to the others, who obeyed him quickly and without question. When the time came to leave, he told Akimbo to walk immediately behind him and not to speak once they set off.

"Keep quiet all the time. Do exactly as I tell you and you'll be all right. Understand?"

Akimbo nodded. The other men were ready now, and they slipped away from the village, following a path that led through the thick grass toward the hills in the distance. Over those hills lay the reserve, and deep in the reserve were the forests where the elephants lived. They were on their way.

\* \* \*

They walked all night. Akimbo was used to walking long distances, but the speed with which the men traveled wore him out. He had to keep up, even though his feet were sore and he longed to lie down in the grass and go to sleep.

By the time the sun rose, they had already crossed into the reserve. Now that it was light, they moved cautiously, keeping to a route that took them through heavy vegetation. Akimbo wondered how long they could keep walking all day as well as all night. When could they sleep?

Suddenly the leader gestured with his hand and the men stopped. "We'll rest here," he said quietly. "Find places to sleep. We'll move again tonight."

Akimbo dropped to the ground underneath the cover of a small thorn bush. The ground was hard but he was so tired that it was more welcome to him than the softest bed. He closed his eyes against the glare of the day and was asleep within seconds.

\*　　\*　　\*

He felt the hand of one of the men on his shoulder.

"Time to go," a voice whispered. "We're leaving."

Akimbo sat up. His body felt sore from sleeping on the ground, and his throat was parched. One of the men gave him a drink of water from a bottle he was carrying. Then he gave him a large piece of dried meat to eat as they walked. The meat was tough and difficult to chew, but Akimbo gnawed at it hungrily.

It was almost dark by the time they set off. They had to travel more slowly now, as the ground was rough and the grass was thick and high. Akimbo had no idea where they were, but he knew that they must be nearing the place where they might expect to find elephants, as he had seen the forests in the distance when they stopped that morning.

They disturbed several wild animals as they made their way. An antelope bounded off from a hollow immediately ahead of them, crashing through the undergrowth in panic. Another large animal was disturbed a little later, and they heard it charging away in the night. It could have been a rhinoceros, and this frightened Akimbo because he knew how dangerous rhinos could be.

They stopped to rest once or twice, and Akimbo found himself less exhausted than on the previous night. At last, toward dawn, they stopped altogether. They were now in heavily wooded land, and at any point they might see elephants. Akimbo assumed that now the hunt was on.

That morning, after resting for three or four hours, the group began to move slowly through the clumps of great trees that broke up the plain. One of the men was now acting as a tracker, and he had picked up the signs of elephants. From time to time he pointed at something on the ground and said something to the man with the limp, who nodded.

Suddenly the tracker stopped. The leader went up to him and crouched beside him. Akimbo and the other men crouched down too, waiting for a sign from the leader.

Akimbo saw the elephants at the edge of the trees. They were moving slowly, browsing among the branches of the trees with their trunks, pulling down clumps of foliage. His heart stopped for a moment. There was a male elephant among them who had a very large pair of tusks—great, white sweeps of ivory. Akimbo knew that the poachers would be bound to go for him.

Suddenly two of the elephants turned to face them. There was a ripple of activity among the others as the two large bulls flapped out their ears and lifted their trunks in the direction of the crouching men. Akimbo realized that the animals had caught their scent and were now alarmed. And if they were alarmed, then they might charge.

The leader gestured to one of the other men, who ran up to him with a rifle. The elephant must have seen the movement because he suddenly moved forward several paces and let out a bellow. Behind him, the other elephants had moved for protection into the shadows of the trees.

Akimbo had never seen a charging elephant, and he was not ready for the speed with which it moved. For a few moments he

was frozen in terror, his eyes fixed on the great creature that was charging toward them. Then, quite suddenly, the elephant stopped. For a short while it stood still, its ears out, its body quivering, small eddies of dust around its feet, and then, without warning, it turned aside and moved back toward the herd.

As this was happening, the leader was fumbling with the rifle. By the time he had it to his shoulder, the elephants had disappeared into the thickness of the forest. Akimbo felt all the fear drain out of his body. They were safe. And so were the elephants—at least, for the time being.

# Escape

The leader was clearly angry over what had happened. He called his men over to him and spoke sharply to them, pointing to where the herd had been to underline his words. They all knew the elephants would move quickly, now that they had scented danger, and it would be difficult to catch up with the herd.

For a few minutes the leader seemed uncertain what to do. Then he spoke.

"We'll follow them. I want to get those tusks."

One of the men stepped forward. "But they're going west. There are rangers that way. It would be too dangerous. They might—"

The leader interrupted him abruptly. "I want those tusks. If you're frightened, you can go home now."

The man looked down. "I'm not frightened."

Akimbo listened. The possibility of traveling west excited him. In that direction lay the ranger camp, and home, and this would make it easier for him to carry out his plan.

With the tracker in the front, his eyes glued to the ground, the line of poachers snaked its way through the thick savannah. Tracking elephants was much easier than tracking other animals, since elephants destroy so much as they make their way, but even so it took all the tracker's skill.

By late afternoon there was still no sign of the elephants, and Akimbo wondered what they would do when darkness fell. It would be impossible to follow the herd any farther— and dangerous, too, as they could suddenly find themselves in the middle of the herd in the darkness, and they would stand no chance then.

When the light became too bad to go on, the leader called his men to a halt. Everybody was tense, weary, and thirsty, and they were pleased to be able to rest.

"We will spend the night here. At first light we can go on."

"But we're too close to the ranger camp," one of the others said. "It's only one or two hours that way."

Akimbo looked where the main pointed. Then, without bothering to hear the leader's answer, he walked off and lay beneath a nearby bush, curling up as if to sleep. The other men all settled themselves too, concealing themselves beneath branches or bushes, and soon anybody walking past would not have realized that five men and a boy were sleeping there.

But the boy was not asleep. Although his bones ached with tiredness, Akimbo fought back the waves of drowsiness and he struggled to keep his mind on what he had to do. At last, when he was sure that all the others were fast asleep, he crept out from underneath his sheltering place.

Nobody moved. Nor did anybody stir as he began to move off in the direction of the ranger camp, which one of the men had pointed out.

"I hope he was right," he said to himself. "If he's not . . ." But Akimbo did not allow himself to think about that. For the moment he knew exactly what he had to do, and he concentrated all his energy on doing it.

It was more frightening than Akimbo could ever have imagined. The moon was behind a cloud, and there was very little light. All that he could make out around him were large black shapes—the shapes of trees, bushes, rocks. Akimbo tried to fix his mind on some landmark in order to keep traveling in the right direction, but it was almost impossible to do this in the darkness. The shape that he aimed for would suddenly be lost, or would look different when he approached it, and there was no way of telling that he was not going around in one large circle.

"If I'm just going round and round, I'll come back to where I started from, and I'll walk right into the poachers."

After about fifteen minutes the clouds cleared, and there was a little more light from the sky. Akimbo could now identify an object to aim for in the distance. He could also move faster, as he did not have to worry so much about the ground suddenly giving way over a cliff.

He broke into a run. It was painful to his tired legs, but he managed to push himself. He scratched himself, of course, on thorn bushes and protruding twigs, but he did not mind that. All he wanted now was to reach the ranger camp and safety.

Suddenly Akimbo stopped. His heart was pounding within him, his skin prickling with fear. Had his ears deceived him, or was it . . . Yes. There it was again. It was a roar. Still quite distant, but unmistakably the roar of a lion.

Akimbo looked around him in panic. All he saw were the same dark shapes and shadows of the African night. Lions could be anywhere. They could be watching him at this moment. They could be crouched, ready to pounce.

He shook his head. He would not give up now. He would not look for the nearest tree and try to climb to safety. He had to get home.

# RHINO CHARGE

**M**oving as quietly as he could, Akimbo made his way through the thick scrub bush. It was difficult to travel quietly, though, unless he also went slowly. And if he went slowly, that would make him more likely to be attacked.

He stopped for a moment and listened. The African night is never quiet. There was the sound of insects, a shrill screeching noise that never stopped. It was everywhere—behind him, around him, above him—and it was difficult to make out any other sound. Yet there it was. There was a sound that was different.

Akimbo took a deep breath. For a few

seconds he felt like shouting out, in the hope that somebody might hear him. But he knew that there was nobody about, and shouting could make his situation even worse. He turned around. Did the sound come from behind?

There was silence. Akimbo took another step and then stopped again. He was sure that he had heard something.

"I'm being stalked. That means it's a lion, or maybe a leopard."

The thought of the fierce animal behind him made his skin chill. He looked around for a tree, and he saw one a few yards away in the darkness. "I can climb that. It's not high, but at least it'll give me some protection."

Slowly he moved over to the tree and reached up for the first, lower branches. His arms were weak with fear, but he still felt strong enough to pull himself up off the ground. Then, just as he began to raise himself, he heard a crashing sound behind him. Fear made him let go, and he dropped down in a heap, the wind knocked out of him.

The crashing noise grew louder as the

animal charged through the undergrowth. Akimbo tried to struggle to his feet, but his limbs would not respond. He was paralyzed with fright.

The rhino moved with extraordinary speed. When Akimbo first saw it, it was a dark blur heading straight toward him, and then in no more than a few seconds it had shot past, thundering off beyond the tree.

Akimbo stayed immobile. As the rhino moved off, the crashing sound grew fainter and, after a while, there was quiet again. Akimbo picked himself up and found, to his surprise, that he was unhurt. The rhino must have missed him by inches.

He started to walk again, dazed, over-whelmed by the closeness of his escape. He realized that he must have been following the rhino for a while and that they had both been equally surprised to find one another. When the rhino had eventually seen him, it had charged, but it had really only meant to get away.

Akimbo now felt all his fear leave him. He had survived a trip with poachers; he had survived a charging rhino. He felt strong now, and he knew that he could make it home.

Akimbo was to remember little of the few hours that followed. He walked quickly and tried to keep going in a straight line. He whistled for a while, and he remembered bruising himself against a rock that was hidden in the grass. And then at last there was the supreme moment when he saw the lights away to his left, almost obscured by trees and not in the direction he would have expected them to be. Yet there was only one thing they could be—the lights of the ranger camp.

His parents were already asleep by the time he reached home. His father woke up at the sound of the door opening and got out of bed to see his son stagger in from the night.

"Akimbo! What are you doing here?"

Akimbo took some time to catch his breath. Then, when he could speak, he blurted out his message.

"There's a gang of poachers. They're . . .

They're in the reserve. They're after elephants."

"How on earth do you know?"

Akimbo told him everything. As he spoke, he watched his father's eyes bulge with surprise.

"But what on earth made you do it?" his father asked, half in anger, half in astonishment.

Akimbo did not give him an answer.

"Look, Father, just believe me. They're there. I know where they are. I can take you there."

Akimbo's father looked doubtful. Then he appeared to make up his mind. He told Akimbo to stay where he was while he went off to summon the head ranger. It was up to him to decide what should be done next.

The head ranger listened gravely to Akimbo's story. When he came to the description of how he had taken the ivory from the storeroom, the ranger frowned and looked angry.

"You shouldn't have done that. You know that was stealing."

"But I only wanted to help. I couldn't let the poachers get away with it."

"That's not your job," interrupted the head ranger. "It's not up to you to stop them."

Akimbo was silent. It was so unfair that the poachers could get away with their greed and cruelty and nobody could stop them. Then, when somebody did try, all he got himself into was trouble.

Akimbo looked at his father, silently appealing for help.

"He has more to say," said his father quietly. "I think you should hear him out."

The head ranger nodded, still frowning, but when Akimbo told him of his meeting with Matimba, he smiled and nodded, pleased at getting the first piece of firm evidence against a man whom he had long suspected.

At the end of Akimbo's tale, the head ranger rose to his feet and rubbed his hands together.

Akimbo waited anxiously.

"Thank you. Well done!"

And with those few words, Akimbo knew that everything would be all right. Or rather, it would be all right if they caught the poachers. If they didn't, then he was sure the blame would land fairly and squarely on himself.

The head ranger now gave orders for all the rangers to be woken. They had to be ready to leave the camp within an hour. They would travel on foot, he said, as the last thing he wanted was for the poachers to be given any warning of their presence.

"Can you manage to walk?" he asked Akimbo casually. "You must be a bit tired."

Akimbo swallowed. He doubted whether his legs could carry him any farther, and the sight of his sleeping mat on the floor of their house had been almost too tempting. But he had started this, and he would have to finish it, even if he dropped in his shoes at the end of it all.

"I'm fine," he replied cheerfully. "I can do it."

Ten rangers set off. They were all armed and equipped with everything they needed for a long hike. Akimbo walked beside the head ranger. Immediately behind him was his father, who encouraged him quietly whenever he seemed to be flagging.

He had a good idea of the direction from which he had come. He thought he recognized certain features—the tip of a hill, silhouetted black against the night sky, or a stretch of forest. But it all seemed so similar in the darkness, and he knew that he could be quite wrong.

Just before dawn they stopped. As the light came up over the horizon and the sun painted the hills with red fire, Akimbo gazed around, really puzzled.

"Do you recognize anything?" whispered the head ranger. "Those trees over there? That hill?"

Akimbo shook his head. "It seems so different. Everything seemed larger at night."

The head ranger nodded. "Don't worry. We'll just go forward very slowly. If you see something familiar, tap me on the arm—don't speak."

Slowly they made their way through the

undergrowth. They were as quiet as they could be, but there were twigs underfoot, which cracked as they trod on them. There were branches that swung back with a swishing sound when they bent them. One of the men coughed once or twice in spite of his efforts to suppress it.

Akimbo was sure they were lost. Should he tell the head ranger now that he had no idea where they were, rather than let them waste more time? But just as he was about to attract the head ranger's attention, he saw it.

There had been a cactus very close to where he had lain down and pretended to sleep. And now, he saw it again. It was definitely the same one. There was that missing branch and the piece that bent down instead of up.

He reached out to attract the head ranger's attention.

"That's it," he whispered. "That's where I was."

At a signal from the head ranger, all the rangers dropped to the ground. Then, half crawling and half running, they moved swiftly toward the cactus.

There was nothing—no sign of the poachers at all. The rangers poked around under the bushes. One came across an empty water bottle and held it up for the others to see. Another found a couple of burned-out matches and showed them to the head ranger.

It was now the turn of the ranger who was most skilled at tracking. He walked around the site where the men had camped that night until he was satisfied that he could work out which direction they had followed. Then, just as the poachers' own tracker had done, he set off, following the signs on the ground, stopping from time to time to peer closely at a footprint or a tuft of grass that had been flattened by somebody's boot.

"They're not far away," he said to the head ranger. "Nor are the elephants."

# ELEPHANTS IN DANGER

As they set off along the tracks of the poachers, Akimbo wondered whether they would be in time. Sooner or later the poachers would catch up with the herd of elephants, and once they did, the fate of the elephants with the handsome tusks would be decided. Akimbo did not care so much if the poachers got away—although he wanted them to be caught. What really mattered to him was stopping them from killing that elephant.

And it seemed such a painfully slow chase!

"Can't we go faster?" Akimbo asked his father. "If we don't hurry, they'll have the tusks by the time we get anywhere near them."

Akimbo's father patted his son on the shoulder. "If we go too fast, we'll lose their trail. A tracker needs time."

And so they inched their way onward until the tracker suddenly held his hand up and everybody stood stock-still.

The head ranger moved quietly to the tracker's side. "What is it?" he whispered.

The tracker pointed to the ground.

"They're ten minutes ahead of us," the tracker said. "Look."

He pointed to the print of a man's boot in the soft sand. It was fresh and clear, and the tracker knew that it had been made only minutes before.

The head ranger signaled to his men to advance more carefully. Now they moved even more slowly, watching each footfall, avoiding stones and twigs and anything else that could give their presence away.

They had reached a place where the ground sloped sharply upward. Ahead of them was the brow of a hill, and on the other side of that the ground sloped gently away to a plain.

The elephants were standing at the edge of a large clump of trees. They were foraging, reaching up with curling trunks to the high branches of trees, their ears fanning slowly to keep the flies away. There were several mother elephants with their young, and there, at the edge of the herd, was the magnificent male with his heavy tusks.

The sight of the elephants distracted the rangers. They had not expected to come across them so quickly, and at such close quarters. Nor had they expected to see the poachers so close to them, crouching only forty or fifty yards away.

Akimbo took in the scene in an instant. He saw the leader of the group of poachers half rise to his feet and bring the rifle to his shoulder, waiting for his opportunity to fire the shot that would bring his quarry crashing to the ground.

The seconds ticked past. Akimbo looked around him. Nobody seemed to be doing anything, and he wondered whether the others had seen the leader. If they had not, then there was only one thing for him to do.

From his crouching position, Akimbo shot to his feet and launched himself forward with a yell. He was aware of his father's cry of horror, but he lurched on, waving his arms, heading straight toward the herd of elephants.

There was a sudden rumpus of movement among the elephants. The smaller ones were quickly fussed away by their mothers while the great elephant with the tusks spun, around to face the source of the disturbance. When the large elephant saw Akimbo, his ears flapped out and his trunk went up.

"No!" shouted Akimbo's father. "Akimbo! Stop!"

The poachers burst out of their hiding places and stared at the boy. Their leader rose up and lowered his gun, looking around him in astonishment, uncertain what to do. Then he saw the rangers behind Akimbo and let out a cry of alarm.

The elephant was scenting the air. Akimbo had dropped to the ground and was sheltered behind a small bush. The large elephant had lost sight of him now and was peering in

the direction from which he had been coming. He began to advance, trumpeting a warning as he did so.

Akimbo looked out from behind his hiding place. He could see the bulk of the elephant coming toward him, but he was not sure if it could see him. He knew that he was in great danger, but for some reason he felt quite calm. His father's words came back to him. "The best thing to do is to stay quite still."

And he was right. The elephant took a few more steps forward and then, no longer aware of the presence of the threat, he moved back to the herd and began to lead them off into the trees. As he did so, Akimbo stood up to get a better view of them. The elephant with the large tusks was encouraging the herd to move faster, pushing against one or two of the reluctant ones, urging the others on with swinging movements of his trunk.

Akimbo caught his breath. There were several baby elephants in the herd, and one of them he was sure he had seen before. Yes! There was no doubt about it. It was a baby elephant with a tear in its right ear. So it had been found by the herd, and it was being looked after.

With the elephants dispersed, the rangers turned their attention to the poachers. The leader realized the gang was outnumbered and surrendered himself almost immediately. He was followed by all of his men. They glowered in anger at Akimbo. But Akimbo did not mind. The poachers could do him no harm now.

Akimbo's father seemed too shocked by what had happened to say much to his son on the way back to the camp. After a while, he managed to speak, still trembling.

"You were very, very lucky there. I thought the elephant would get you before we had time to do anything."

"It almost did. But it was the only way I could warn it."

"It was still no reason to take that risk. If you hadn't found that bush to drop behind, I don't know . . ."

"But I *did* find it."

The head ranger, who had been listening to them, now joined in. "You were very brave. If it hadn't been for you, that elephant would have lost its life.''

Back at the camp, the rangers arranged for the police to come out to collect the poachers, and the head ranger had to pass on the information he had received about Matimba. He enjoyed doing this, as it would give him great pleasure to see Matimba arrested and his cruel trade in stolen ivory brought to an end.

But there was only one thing that Akimbo wanted to do. He lay down on his sleeping mat, feeling all the aching tiredness flow out of his weary limbs. Within seconds he was asleep.

He slept for almost twenty hours, and at some point in that long sleep he dreamed. He dreamed of the elephants. He dreamed that he was out on the savannah, watching the elephant with the great tusks walk slowly through the waving, golden grass. And as it walked past, it turned and looked at him. This time it did not prepare to charge, but lifted its trunk, as if to salute Akimbo, its friend. And Akimbo raised his hand to it too, and then watched it walk slowly away.

# Did You Know?

- The elephant is the largest land-dwelling animal. Male elephants can grow to be as tall as eleven feet—more than twice as tall as many adult humans.

- Elephants can weigh as much as a school bus—between ten and fourteen thousand pounds!

- Most elephants live in the grasslands of Africa and in the forests of Asia, in groups called herds. Up to ten females and their young will make up a herd, which is led by the matriarch, the oldest and largest female.

- There are two species of elephant—the Asian elephant and the African elephant. Asian elephants have smaller ears and shorter tusks than African elephants. The African elephant is bigger and taller than the Asian elephant.

- Elephants are plant-eaters. Because they are such big animals, they need to eat large amounts of leaves, grass, and tree bark. They spend as much as sixteen hours a day eating, and they poop about 100 pounds a day!

• Elephants talk to each other by making sounds called "tummy rumbles." They also make a "trumpeting" sound to call to each other.

• Elephants sleep while standing up, although the babies will sometimes lie down to sleep.

• An elephant's ears are covered in veins, which form distinct and unique patterns that can be used to identify individuals—just like human fingerprints.

• Elephants have four teeth and two "tusks." The tusks grow about seven inches a year, and they can reach up to twenty feet long. The tusks are made of ivory, which is very valuable. A great number of elephants have been shot in the past so that people could poach their tusks, but these days very few are killed for their ivory, and there are laws to protect the elephants.

• September 22 is Elephant Appreciation Day.

# AFRICAN WILDLIFE FOUNDATION®

You can learn all about elephants and lions and cheetahs and zebras and giraffes and other wildlife by visiting the African Wildlife Foundation at www.awf.org.

After you learn about the wild animals, you can help save them—by supporting the African Wildlife Foundation.

The African Wildlife Foundation has worked with the people of Africa for forty-five years. They train park rangers, like Akimbo's father, to protect wildlife and catch poachers. They give scholarships to girls and boys like Akimbo so they can grow up and learn to be scientists who protect Africa's mighty rivers and great forests.

# Don't miss any adventure, mystery, and fun with these Alexander McCall Smith titles!

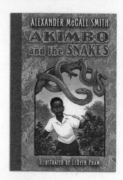

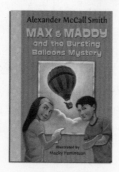

# Now available in paperback!

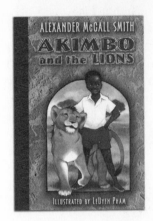

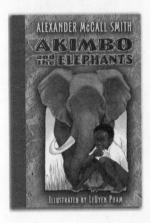

# A Note on the Author

Graham Clark

ALEXANDER MCCALL SMITH
has written more than fifty
books, including the *New York
Times* bestselling No. 1 Ladies'
Detective Agency mysteries and
The Sunday Philosophy Club
series. A professor of medical law
at Edinburgh University, he was
born in what is now Zimbabwe
and taught law at the University
of Botswana. He lives in
Edinburgh, Scotland.

Visit him at WWW.ALEXANDERMCCALLSMITH.COM

# A Note on the Illustrator

LEUYEN PHAM is the illustra-
tor of numerous award-winning
books for children including *Big
Sister, Little Sister* (which she also
wrote); *Sing-Along Song*; and
*Piggies in a Polka*. She lives in San
Francisco, California.

Mark Mulgrew

Visit her at WWW.LEUYENPHAM.COM